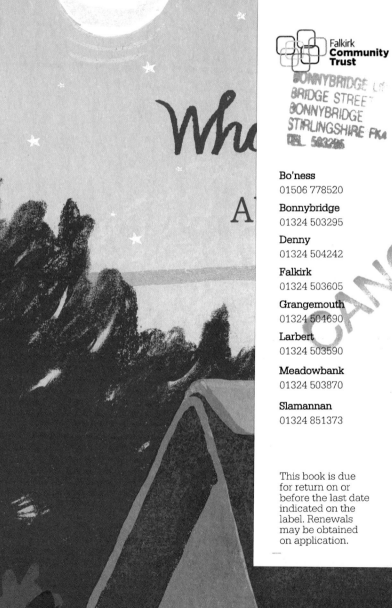

PUFFIN

D0193237

For Sophie, who wouldn't
go to bed – A.L.

For Gordon, Em and Joe – E.C.

PUFFIN BOOKS

UK | USA | Canada | Ireland | Australia
India | New Zealand | South Africa
Puffin Books is part of the Penguin
Random House group of companies
whose addresses can be found at
global.penguinrandomhouse.com.
www.penguin.co.uk
www.puffin.co.uk
www.ladybird.co.uk

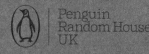
Penguin
Random House
UK

First published 2019
001

Text copyright © Abie Longstaff, 2019
Illustrations copyright © Eve Coy, 2019
The moral right of the author and
illustrator has been asserted

Printed in China

A CIP catalogue record for this book is
available from the British Library

ISBN: 978-0-141-37456-7

All correspondence to:
Puffin Books
Penguin Random House Children's
80 Strand, London WC2R 0RL

MIX
Paper from
responsible sources
FSC® C018179

The stars are out,
the moon is bright . . .

Who's going to bed?

The pirates are going to bed.
They've packed away their treasure,
folded up their flag
and are settling down in their hammocks.
Sleep tight, pirates.

Shhhh!

Who's going to bed?

The animals are going to bed.
They've eaten their greens, curled up their trunks
and are resting their heads.
Sleep tight, animals.

Shhhh!

Who's going to bed?

The teddies are going to bed.
They've finished their picnic,
packed away their blanket
and are cuddled up in their cottage.
Sleep tight, teddies.

Shhhh!

Who's going to bed?

The king and queen are going to bed.
They've taken off their crowns,
tucked in their knights
and are snoozing on their silk pillows.
Sleep tight, royals.

Shhhh!

Who's going to bed?

Everyone is
going to bed!

But wait!
What's this?
Someone is
still **awake** . . .

It's a cheeky baby!
He's not going to bed.

He's off on an adventure.
There he goes!

Past the castle . . .
Wake up! Wake up! BANG BANG BANG!

Past the cottage . . .
Wake up! Wake up! CRASH CRASH CRASH!

Past the jungle . . .
Wake up! Wake up! TOOT TOOT TOOT!

Past the ship . . .
Wake up! Wake up! YO HO HO!

Now no one is going to bed!
Everyone is off on an adventure!

On crawls
the cheeky baby . . .

But wait!
What's this?

It's a little dragon!
Is she off on an adventure too?

NO!
She's a sleepy little dragon.

She wants to go to bed.

But everyone is being far too noisy.

Poor little dragon.

She's SO tired!

But wait!
What's this?
The cheeky baby stops.
He claps his hands together
and says:

SHHHH!

So very, very quietly . . .

very, very gently . . .

the knights carry
the dragon to bed . . .

the king and queen
tuck her in . . .

the teddies find
a blankie . . .

the monkeys read a story . . .

the pirates sing
a lullaby . . .

and the baby kisses her goodnight.
Sleep tight, little dragon.

Shhhh!

The dragon gives a big yawn.

Then the knights, the king and the queen start to yawn.
So do the teddies
and the animals
and the pirates!

Everyone is sleepy now, especially the baby.
His is the **biggest** yawn of all.

YAWWWN!

He wants to go to bed.

So the pirates
sail him . . .

the animals
swing him . . .

the teddies
carry him . . .

and the knights
march him . . .

. . . all the way home to bed.

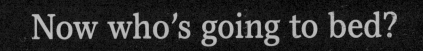

Now who's going to bed?